it all started with a dream
of a sun.
not just of a sun,
but a blue sun, bright teint
to the point of a jazz mood. And seeing
~~to the point~~ here were clouds in
~~the clouds~~ outline. ~~And~~ Nothing

THANK YOU to Geoffrey Chandler,
for a lifetime's worth of being a best friend
in all of the crazy phases of life we've
been through together. from newspaper
co-workers to video game nerds to dads to
... this?
look at us!

THANK YOU to the Charleston County
Library Staff for feeding my new obsession
with novels in verse.

THANK YOU to Natasha Akery,
Jane Akery, Eleanor Akery, Halley Repasch,
Marjory Wentworth, and
Kwame Alexander for sitting with this
story before it was complete.
your attention to my work is valuable to
me, beyond any award i've been given.
thank you.

& THANK YOU (yes, you!)
for being here.

this book was made
by a human, so there will be mistakes.
(i celebrate them!).
- marcus

1

THE COLOR OF CARINA'S DREAMS

MARCUS AMAKER

WITH ART BY **GEOFFREY CHANDLER**

The author is available for performances and writing workshops.
If interested, please email **marcus@marcusamaker.com**.

Library of Congress Control Number: Applied for

ISBN (Paperback): 979-8-9934361-1-1
ISBN (Digital PDF): 979-8-9934361-0-4

Printed in the United States of America.
First printing edition 2025.

Library of Congress Subject Headings:
Amaker, Marcus - Fiction.
Dreams - Fiction.
Friendship - Fiction.
Young adult fiction - Novels in verse.

Title font: Softie Marker
Text font: Georgia Pro

Published by Free Verse Press
Free Verse, LLC
North Charleston, South Carolina
charlestonpoets.com

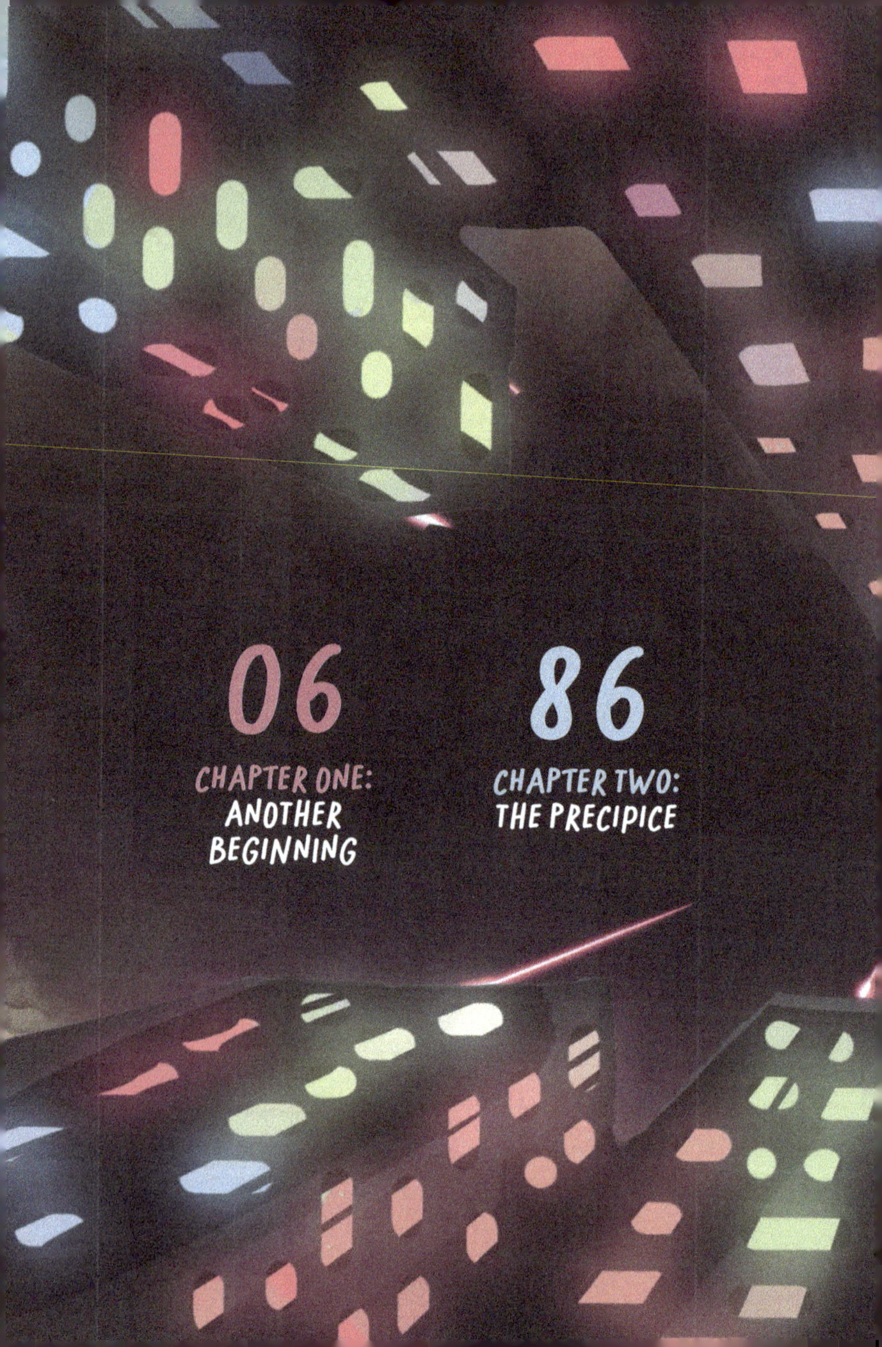

160

CHAPTER THREE:
TRANSFORMATION

CHAPTER ONE:
ANOTHER BEGINNING

IT ALL STARTED WITH A DREAM

of a sun.
not an ordinary sun,
but a *blue* sun, brightened
like a moody jazz album cover.

and the clouds
were just
thin outlines
of shapes
that overlapped
in an empty sky.

i remember looking down
and my feet were not there.

was i flying?
was i floating?
was i a dragonfly?

MAYBE ALL OF THE ABOVE

because
i saw wings
on both sides
of me,

tracing faint circles
in an air that was
comforting,
warm with sound,

and holding
me in place.

I'LL NEVER FORGET.

it wasn't scary at all.
it was beautiful and strange.
and completely still.

it was a little weird
to feel grounded
even though
i wasn't
touching the ground
at all.

that was the first one
i remember.

the first dream,
i mean.

(ANOTHER DETAIL)

the sky
felt like
water!

THE JOURNAL

i don't dream every night.
sometimes the dark
just stays dark,

and i am completely
cool with that.

but when my dreams come,
they are awesome!

they feel like
sparkly little gifts
from the stars.

i use them as fuel
to make art,

which all goes
in my messy
blue journal.

IT'S IN YOUR CLOTHES NOW.

i'm one of the few
people i know
who has a journal.

(a *paper* journal,
i mean).

everything
is so digital.

there is code
in our clothes.

there is code
in the sky.

i felt it was
important
to try and keep
some things
to myself.

A DREAM COMES TRUE

a new device
was just announced -

something called
'dreamkastr'
that can apparently
record your dreams!

if you dream
in full color,
it will show it back to you.

it can also
somehow capture
and record
the *sounds*
of the dream.

and you can save it
or play it back
whenever you want!

dream devices have
been in the works
for a long time now,

and i think i want one.
.... ok, i *know* i want one.

bad.

THE FORMLESS

getting a dreamkastr
is all i can think about,
actually.

for so long,
my dreams have been
my personal
and delightfully weird
safe space
to play.

and it's all
in my head.

i'll still journal
if i get a dreamkastr,
but this literally
changes everything!

HOME IS A FLOWER

i live with
my mama jeanie
and mama zara.

they are my rock
and provide
such incredible
love.

despite the
radical change
after the war,

they've been
able to mentally
get it together
and constantly
provide love
and support
for whoever i am
or whatever i need.

MAMA ZARA'S HANDS

always smell
like metal
because of
her garage.

she fixes things
most people throw away -
headphones, old devices,
a cracked tablet
from the 21st century,
before the great leap.

"there was so much
waste back then,"
she says.
"and there's a story
in every wire
if you're patient enough
to listen."

MAMA JEANIE'S RHYTHM

mama jeanie still dances
in the mornings,

bare feet on cool tile,
a quiet rhythm
that keeps
the house
breathing.

performance
is her passion.

she's been a dancer
since she was 7 years old.

she teaches
improvisational dance
at a local
studio.

A CONSTELLATION NAMED ME

mama zara told me,
"your name is carina,
after the constellation.

it means 'keel,'
the part of a ship
that keeps it steady.

you're steady too,
even when you don't feel it."

sometimes i look up
and try to find my name
in the night sky.

some of my friends
changed their name,
and i love them for that.

but i'm going to keep mine.

A DREAM COMES TRUE (AGAIN)

one morning
before breakfast
i started looking
through my journal.

there are stickers
everywhere
of my favorite bands.

and i have a maya-zen
sticker on there, too!

anyway, just
as i was closing the journal,
mama zara walks in
and hands it to me:

a dreamkastr!

WHAT SHE SAYS AS SHE HANDS IT TO ME

"here you are, love,"
mama zara says,
her clothes brushing mine
as she sits on my bed.

the faint smell
of a soldering tool
still lingers
on her black hair.

i love that she
continued
the passion she had
for objects
when she was a kid.

at 10, she started
building robots.

"i know how much
you've wanted one.

remember,
it's cool for you
to get on this,

but don't let it
get on you."

"cool!"
i say as i take
the dreamkastr
from her hands.

MORNING RUSH

i barely eat breakfast.
the cereal turns soggy
while i stare
at the small golden disc
in front of me.

it feels like
the dreamkastr
already knows me.

i should be brushing my teeth,
finding socks,
getting my things together.

but all i can think about
is what tonight
will be like
when i go
to sleep with
a dreamkastr
for the first time.

will i dream?

if so, it would be incredible
to play it all back
in color
tomorrow morning.

THE LITTLE DOME

it fits
in the palm of my hand -
round, smooth,
gold like a sunrise.

when i tilt it,
it glows
across its edges.

it can match
the color of
whatever surface
it rests on -
journal blue,
the dark green of my desk,

or the brown
of my own skin.

press it and
the warmest chime
you've ever heard
plays before a screen pops up
above it with all of
the dreams,
right there. in motion.

almost like
a cute little
digital chameleon.

SCHOOL

somehow
i make it
out of the door
for the walk
to school.

i can't wait
to tell maya-zen
and valyn
about my new
little toy.

MAYA-ZEN, VALYN, & I

are a galaxy of our own.

we do everything together.
we recently started a
music club.

the members?
just us.

(old vinyl records - not
digital. maya-zen wouldn't
have it any other way! they say
digital sound loses soul.)

we've been to
a few concerts together,
we play video games,
we ride bikes
"outside" ....

"OUTSIDE"

isn't really outside,
you know. it's a joke
between us. every time
we say "outside," we put
quotes around it
because of the climate dome.

3044

"life in the
31st century
is crazy.
i'm not sure
our ancestors
wanted this,"
said maya-zen once,

half-smiling,
half-staring
at the ground.

they are probably right.

holograms float
through the air
like ghosts
with too much confidence.

machines hum
a constant lullaby,
and even the stars
feel further away.

WE SLEEP UNDER CODE.

we live beneath
the climate dome
because the sky changed.

a thin translucent layer
with tiny bits of code -

you can still see rain
fall through it.

the sunlight slides
through it
and raindrops slip
between the patterns
of data,
rewriting themselves
on the way down.

but there have been
many, many issues
with it.

it was once cracked
by lightning.

and one time
it rebooted itself
on its own.

PRETENDING

"protecting us
from the permanent change
in the atmosphere"
is what they said.

a promise
that seemed to be
printed on every wall
and screen.

they said it would hover
through the clouds -

sometimes above them,
sometimes below -

always working,
always filtering,
always watching.

at night
you can see it shimmer,

a busy ring
around our world,
pretending
to be sky.

BREATH / BREATHE

sometimes,
i imagine
the *whole thing*
cracking open.

sunlight spilling
through the fractures,
reminding us
what the real sky
feels like.

i'd love to one day
feel the fresh air,
like my
ancestors.

they knew a change
was coming,
but they still had
the opportunity
to breathe in

natural air.

WHILE LOOKING UP

sometimes
i see a family of birds
making a nest in a tree

underneath
this thin thing

that they can
somehow fly through
without any harm.

i wonder if the birds
are actually aware of it?

or maybe,
to them,
this is just
another unnatural
strange human-made thing

that they are
forced to accept?

MAYA-ZEN

thinks the climate dome
is actually bad for us. "i don't
trust the code. something
about it is very weird to me,"
they say, with focused,
but gentle,
brown eyes.

they also have
no interest in a dreamkastr.

maya-zen and their family are
"old school." they listen to records,
read books (on paper!), and don't
do social media.

maya-zen doesn't have many friends,
but they are completely fine with that.

oh, and they make
weird music (in a good way).

they are one of the smartest,
tender, and most mysterious
people i know.

.WAV

maya-zen once told me
that silence
has its own temperature.

they collect it.
archive it.

listen to the quiet
between centuries.

they use the sound archive
to collect clips of
people talking,
or walking on leaves.

their room is a museum
of .wav files -

old smartphones
that still hold
the laughter of 2025,

tiny data fossils
from before the world
became so loud.

"i like to hear
what the world sounded like
in the old days,"
they say.

VALYN

is also my bestie.
he is one of the funniest
people i know.

he has a gentle
heart. but here's
the funny thing:

valyn has the most
boring dreams
i've ever seen or heard of!

he literally dreams about
washing the dishes.

"true art is subjective."
he said, with a smile,
in class one day.

as a joke,
he also got a dreamkastr.
the first dream he shared with us
was one where he was
alphabetizing
a bookshelf.

he showed it to us,
and we laughed
and laughed.

CONNECTING THE DOTS

it seems like
valyn's mind
is always
building something.

levels,
mazes,
jokes in his head,
entire worlds
made of pixels.

he says coding
feels like gardening -
you plant an idea,
wait for it to grow,
then clear the bugs
like weeds.

he laughs easy,
but stays steady -

the kind of friend
who doesn't drift
when the rest of us do.

sometimes i envy
how he sees
the beauty in code.

THE SILENCE BETWEEN THE WORDS

we are the type of friends
who believe that
conversation
isn't the best way
to interact with each other,

it's funny to me
that people
automatically
start talking when
they see each other.

like,

can't we just
be together first,

without awkward
greetings?

anyway,
that's maya-zen,
valyn, & i.

we can be silent together
and be completely
comfortable.

i love it.

THE HALLWAY CURRENT

my school's hallways
are a chaotic melody
of tired teenagers
staring at
their fingers
and the bright
holographic displays
that flow from
their fingertips.

valyn floats ahead,
navigating the crowd
like he owns it,
his thick locs bouncing
with the energy
that is in his body.

maya-zen walks beside me,
their headphones on,
their fingers drumming a beat
only they can hear.

i'm clutching my bag
and obsessively checking
for my journal and my dreamkastr,
trying not to get swept away
in the current of it all

as we make our way
to history class.

WHAT WE STUDY NOW

our school systems
start and end
with studying emotions.

textbooks sparkle
with empathy maps
for the land

and energy maps
for the body.

showing where
sorrow begins,

where forgiveness
can take root.

i think of my ancestors,
placing medicine bottles
next to meditation stones,

holding mental health
with gentle hands,

standing up
to old traditions

and i whisper
a thank you.

HISTORY CLASS: THE YEAR 2077

"life on our planet
was different
before the great leap,"
our teacher says,
his voice echoing through
the digital amphitheater.

"2077 happened.
and after the war,
humanity evolved
to a level of compassion
never seen before.

a hologram blooms in front of us
and shows the story
of the woman
who first made contact
with a radiant figure,
a being from beyond our galaxy.

"we received knowledge,"
he continues,
"that eradicated bodily diseases,
and rewired our understanding
of existence.

but,
quite understandably,
not everyone
believed."

THE SHIFT

"a war broke out.
those who followed
the teachings
became the new foundation tribe,
the very stone of our society."

i glance at the history datapad
in front of me,
then at the climate dome
above our city.

i wonder if the
beings knew we'd
someday need
a climate dome
to hover above
our cities?

did anyone ever
really listen to
each other before
going to war?

humans are strange.

i wonder if the beings
ever regretted making contact?

maybe that's why
they disappeared again.

THIS PAGE IS A MIRROR

i grab my journal and write:

"what would they say
if they could
see us now?

the ones who lived
before all of this.

would they envy us
and our too-fast
technology,

or pity us
for the way we
let it define
everything?"

FIELD RECORDING (3044)

during lunch,
valyn is staring
at the screen
rising from his
finger.

we are all
on a bench
"outside."

"history is always
so heavy," says valyn,
not moving his eyes
from the hologram
that's busy with code.

maya-zen
walks the edge
of the school
with a small recorder,

capturing birds,
raindrops,
the wind
and its relationship
with trees.

they say it's
"for the album."

BACK HOME

the sky buzzes
as school lets out.

valyn and maya-zen
peel off toward home,

their laughter echoing
like afterthoughts
in the air.

the streets are lined
with holograms.
a drone shines overhead,
delivering somebody's dinner.
children chase its shadow,
laughing.

mama jeanie's voice
is the first thing i hear
when i open the door.

she and mama zara say,
"tell us about your day"
and i'll say "fine,"

but i think they both know
all i want to think or talk about
is my dreamkastr
and our first night
together.

BLINKING IN TIME

how do you capture
what can't be touched?

something about
the lights.

the technology
is somehow
... in the lights?

i go to bed early,
and place it
right next to me.

a steady pulse
blinks in time
with my heartbeat.

i write in my journal
on most nights.

tonight's entry was one line:
"tonight, i give my mind
and my dreams
permission
to just be."

i fall asleep.

MULTIPLE MOONS (BLINK)

i had a lucid dream
that felt strangely familiar.

there were
four pink moons
in a dark,
but comforting sky.

large, round, balls
casting a soft,
slightly cold
glow to anyone
who looked at them.

i was a blackbird.

one time i blinked,
opened my eyes,
and the moons
were above me,
in a single line.

the next time
i blinked,
they shifted
texture
and their
positions
in a
swirly sky.

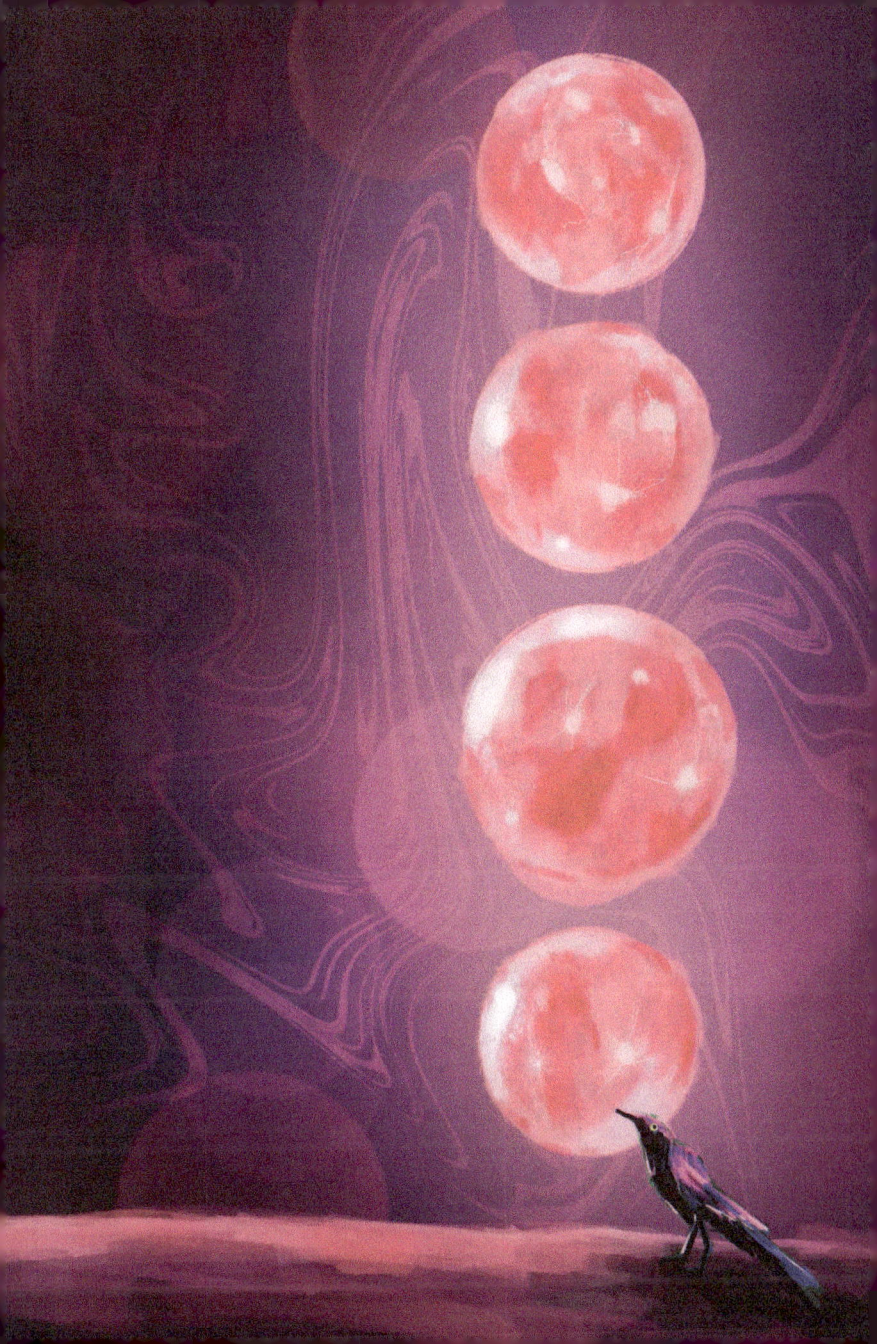

MORNING

i wake up smiling -
the kind of smile
that starts in your chest.

the room is shining,
faint gold,
as if the dreamkastr
is still breathing.

i don't remember
every single detail,
but i'm comforted
by the fact that
somewhere inside
that little circle,

my dream is captured
and waiting
to be seen again.

i can't wait to see
maya-zen
and valyn
today to tell them
and ... show them?

i put the dreamkastr
in my bag
and head to school.

THE WEIGHT OF LIGHT

i have to admit,
sometimes
dreamkastr
feels like
the potential
of pure magic.

it's a mirror
that remembers me -
something i can
always go back to.

all the colors that flash
behind my eyes
when the world
sleeps.

it doesn't judge.

it just keeps them safe,
ready to replay when i need
to remind myself
of who i am.

ANTICIPATION ...

that
weird and
strange dream
is echoing
in my brain.

and i have it
all on my dreamkastr!

i can't wait
to show them.

they'll lose their minds.

i've never seen
four moons
before.

i've never seen
a sky like that before.

SMALL THING

on the walk to class
a leaf
spins down
in a slow
gentle way,

landing
right on top
of my shoe.

i pause,
just long enough
to breathe,

and remember
i'm still
a *person*
before
i'm a post.

MORNING ORBIT

maya-zen's
headphones are a lush blue.

valyn's laugh
ricochets off the lockers.
we move through the halls
like satellites -

each with our own gravity,
each pulled toward
the same center.

i check my bag again,
fingers itching to press play
on last night's dream.

"i'll meet you
at lunch,"
i say,

trying not
to float away
with excitement.

VINTAGE TECH

room 1123 smells
like dust and static.

rows of old devices
blink quietly -

tiny ghosts
from before
the great leap.

each screen
holds a thousand faces
that will never look up again.

we call it
a museum of lost moments,

but it feels
like a mirror
of everything
we forget
on purpose.

OUR LUNCHTIME ORBIT

our table feels like a planet
with its own gravity.

as we all sit down
with our food,
we each settle
into the funny little roles
we've made for ourselves:

maya-zen taps out beats
and is making us laugh
with weird sounds they got
from manipulating
people's voices.

through all of that,
valyn is halfway paying attention,
sketching game characters
on his datapad,
his head full of worlds
no one has played yet.

i used to make fun
of him for being on it
so much, but now i totally get it.

i can't think of anything else
but my dreamkastr
and the strange dream
i had last night.

POCKET GLOW

"ok, you all.
you have to see this,"
i say, handing valyn
my dreamkastr.

maya-zen leans over,
curious.

i pull it out of my bag
and the disc
calmly lights up.

a screen emerges above it.
i move my hand over it
and it expands in front of us.

and there it is,
ready to be played:

the stars, the colors,
the blackbird.

the moons shifting,
blinking,

the strange,
mysterious glow
that i still feel ...

HOW STRANGE ...

to
see
a
thing
from
my
head
come
to
life
right
in
front
of
me
in
full
color (!)

SILENCE

valyn is
speechless
and maya-zen
just stares.

the dream unfolds:
every detail
playing out
like it did
behind my eyes.

when it's over,
they're still quiet.

i wonder if
they didn't like it?

THE STORYTELLER

"that was incredible,"
valyn says finally,
his voice hushed
like we're in a library.

"carina, you're like -
a storyteller
of the subconcious.
a total star,"
says maya-zen.

their words
stay with me.

AND SOMEONE ELSE SAYS

"is that
a dreamkastr?

how do you
even dream
like that?
it's like ...

you're creating
art in your sleep!"

i didn't realize
a crowd
started to form
around us
after i
pressed play.

PASSING IT AROUND

my dreamkastr makes
its rounds,
from valyn to maya-zen,
and then to
others at our table.

i sit back, watching
their faces -
the way their eyes light up,
the way they lean closer.

it feels good,
but also strange,
to see my dream
played over
and over
again ...

THE FIRST FANS

someone says,
"you have
to check this out."

the table next to us turns,
craning their necks to see.
another person comes over,
then another,

then another.

THE FIRST CROWD

it happens faster than i expect.
the lunchroom fills
with whispers and gasps.

i watch as my dream
draws a crowd,
each person leaning closer
to the screen.

THE FIRST TIME

for the first time,
people i barely know
are looking at me
like i'm someone
worth noticing.

it's unsettling -
this attention,
this sudden interest
in what i can do

and not
who i am.

VALYN'S JOKE

"this is wild,"
valyn says,
grinning.

"carina,
you're like
a celebrity now."

i roll my eyes,
but the thought
lingers.

DIFFERENT

as the crowd grows,
maya-zen
leans close to me.

"does this
feel weird to you?"
they whisper.

i nod, but i can't
explain why.

"it's not bad, i guess -
it's just... different."

I DON'T HAVE ANY ANSWERS.

"can you help me dream like this?"
"do you do it on purpose?"
"can you teach me?""

SAGITTARIUS A*

by the end of lunch,
i'm the center of attention.

it's not like before,
when some people teased me
for being "the dream girl."

this is different.
this feels like respect,

but it also feels fragile.

UNLIKELY STAR

walking to class
with my dreamkastr
in my bag,

i hear my name
on people's lips.

with curiosity.
admiration, even.

it's strange
to feel seen,

but i kind
of like it ...

TOO BRIGHT

in homeroom,
valyn nudges me.

"are you okay?"
he asks,
and i nod.

but inside,
i'm spinning.

dreams have always
been mine,
a private escape.

i feel a rush
of excitement
and a little bit
of anxiety
in my stomach.

is this
what a spotlight
feels like?

SAFE SPACE

coming home
felt great

and i slipped out
of a costume
too grand for me to wear.

even though
the spotlight lingered,
the heat from it
is not too hot
when i'm at home.

i close
the bedroom door
behind me

and the crowd,
the voices,
the echoes

are all quiet
now.

MAMA JEANIE'S ARMS

mama jeanie finds me
sitting on the edge of the bed,
my dreamkastr still warm
in my hand.

she smells
like fancy soap,
cocoa butter
and lemon.

her movements
are slow, deliberate -

every gesture a memory
of a stage
that doesn't
exist anymore.

"talk to me," she says,
her voice low, steady,
like the ground under my feet
when i feel like i'm falling.

so i do.

"today felt ... strange.
but i feel better now,"
i say.

MAMA ZARA'S WISDOM

mama zara joins us,
her hands warm on my shoulders.

"carina, your light is your own.
no one else gets to claim it.

people might try
to pull pieces of you,
but you decide
what to give away."

her words land softly,
but they stuck with me
all night.

she once told me
she doesn't trust machines
that can't break.

"humans are flawed,
and that is the beauty
of our species.
we shouldnt be
trying to make
perfect things."

"everything real,"
she says,
"needs repair
sometimes."

A MOMENT TOGETHER

we sit in silence
for a while,
the three of us.

mama jeanie
places her right hand
on my back
and gently
runs her fingers
up and down my spine.

and mama zara looks up
like she can see the stars
through the ceiling.

i lean into them,
and for a moment,
everything feels simple again.

THE JOURNAL

after they leave,
i open my journal.
its cover worn smooth
from years of use.

the pages smell like ink
and memory.

i run my fingers
over old entries,
moments that once felt
so urgent
and so big
when they
were happening.

and i realize,
this is just
a *new* moment
that i will
eventually get over.

JUST ON PAPER

i flip through the journal slowly,
stopping at sketches of dreams
i barely remember now.

a sky full of ribbons,
a garden of crystal trees,
a house where every room
was a different color of light,
and more
and more
and more.

i really wish
i had my dreamkastr
back then.

because now -
alone,
in the quiet of my room,
i would love
to relive
those moments.

to watch them
playing in front of me,
reminding me
of my gift.

INTO SLEEP

that night,
i fall asleep clutching the journal
on my chest,
its weight grounding me
to the bed
like an anchor.

the dreamkastr
is beside me
on my desk,
absorbing and changing
into the color of the
white paper beneath it.

that night,
dreams come quickly,
filling my mind with colors
and shapes
that don't belong
to the waking world.

i don't fight them.
i let them carry me away.

WARMTH

a river opened
inside my chest.

i floated up
through the night sky.

night stars leaned closer,
their energy warm,
somehow telling me
i was not alone.

LOVE FEELS LIKE

i was a star
that could shoot
across the galaxy.

and every time
i zipped through
the big black sky,
a gorgeous green light
surrounded me.

i eventually made it
to a cluster
of what must have been
a thousand stars.

each star
had its own
unique color.

and when
i got close to them,
we all melted
into one
large light.

it felt like love.

or what i hope
love feels like.

(ANOTHER DETAIL)

it felt like
what my
mama jeanie
describes
when she
talks about
dancing.

i woke up
crying
happy
tears.

A NEW START

i woke up
feeling lighter,
the dreams still buzzing
at the edges of my mind.

dreamkastr sits there,
its screen dark,
but i know
it saw everything.

these dreams
feel too big
to explain,
but i don't
have to.

THE UPDATE

a gentle chime
wakes me.

the chime is
not my alarm,
but the dreamkastr.

it blinks
a tiny pulse of gold.

"update complete,"
it says,
like a whisper
from another world.

i smile,
half-awake,
half-still in the dream,

wondering
what could possibly
be new.

CONNECTED

"dreamkastr is now
part of the global network."

the words hover
in the air above the screen,

slowly unfolding
like flower petals.

for a moment,
i just watch -

the calm pulse,
the quiet promise
of connection.

if my dreams
can travel farther
than i can,

maybe that's
a kind of magic too.

part of me likes the idea
of sharing these dreams.
another part
isn't so sure.

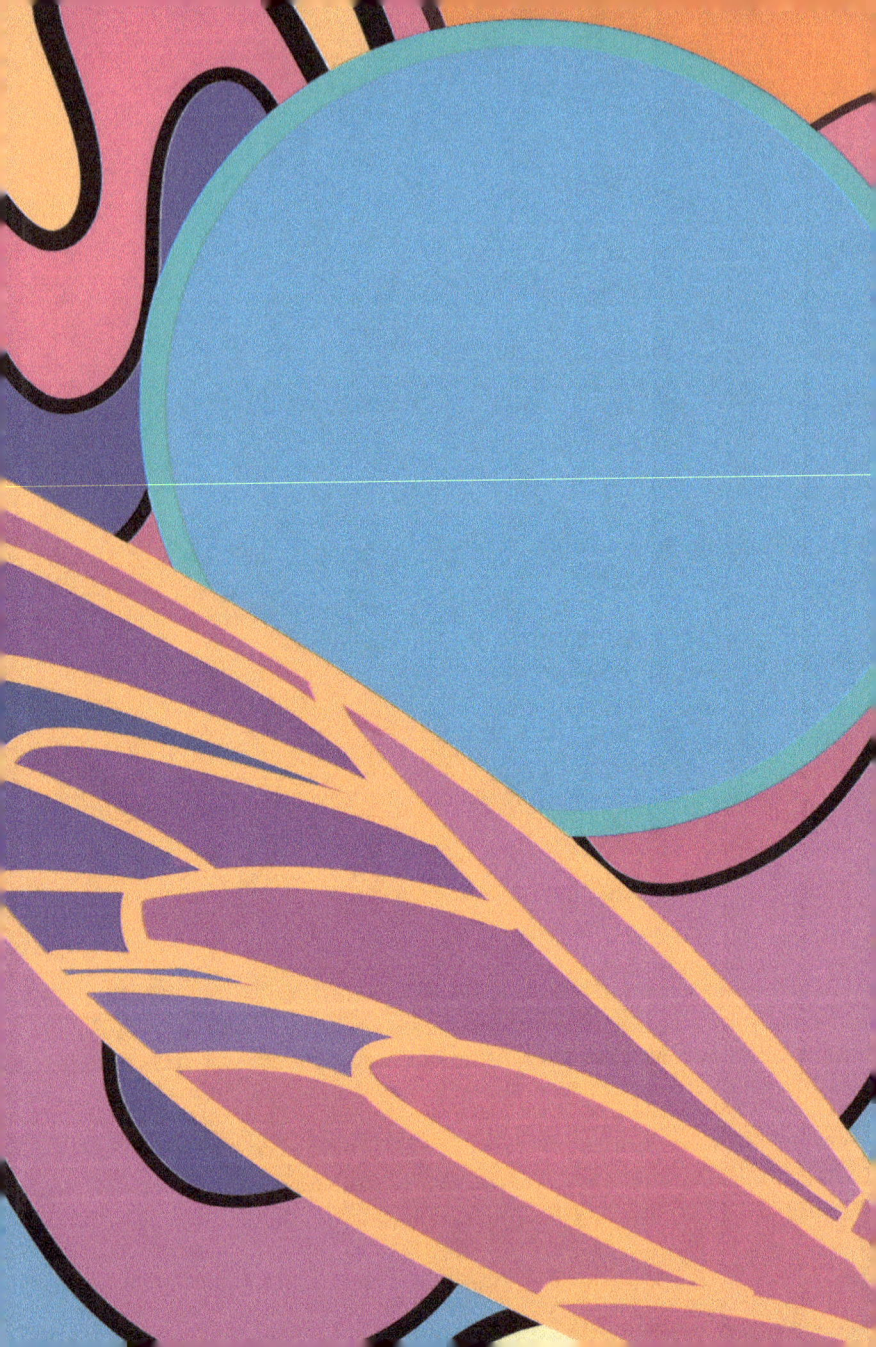

CHAPTER TWO:
THE PRECIPICE

44 DAYS LATER ...

HOW DREAMS ARE CAPTURED

at night, it blinks,
quiet as confession,
threading through our rooms -
just a pulse
in the ceiling,
a rhythm we ignore.

when i close my eyes,
the light slides in,
gentle as a whisper,
mapping my mind.

they say it's safe,
a silent capture.

a flicker in the dark that slips
under my eyelids, scooping up scenes
i don't even remember.

by morning, it holds them,
my nocturnal secrets,
pressed and
flowing like fireflies in a jar,
ready to release
to whoever
wants to see.

PLAY

pressing the dreamkastr
on any surface
brings up the dream
as a clear
hologram.

watching them
feels like a familiar story
waiting to be told
for the first time.

watching them play
feels like opening a door,
letting my friends wander in,
sit in the wonder
of my dreaming,

seeing the world
through my eyes
like we are holding hands
in the dark.

MIRROR SELVES

in my dreams
i am louder,
braver,
whole.

sometimes
i wonder
which version
is the real me -

the one who flies
through galaxies
and touches stars
at nighttime,

or the one
who can't
make eye contact
in the hallway
at school
during the day.

MORNING PULSE

the dome
looms overhead,

a constant reminder
of the times we
are in,

maya-zen
skips every third crack,

valyn gives
us his trademark smile.

the city feels awake today,
but slower somehow -

like we're part of its rhythm,
not racing it.

we talk in fragments,
half-jokes,
our laughter floating
like lingering static

UPDATE CHATTER

we don't even call it the "update" anymore.

it's just what life does now -
our dreams
automatically go public
before breakfast.

valyn scrolls through
other people's dreams
while we walk,

laughing with someone
who dreamt
about flying to math class
in a shoebox.

maya-zen shakes their head.

"it's weird," they say,
"watching people sleep together
but apart."

i don't answer,
but i realize
they make
a good point.

TIMELINE OF SLEEP

the feed is busy.
it is a collage
of everyone's midnights -

bright, strange,
sometimes too real.

there's comfort in it,
seeing the world dream
in the same rhythm.

some clips loop in my mind -

a city breathing underwater,

a child chasing a star,

a stranger whispering poetry.

it's beautiful,
but also
a little crowded
in my head.

@pixeldust94: simply incredible, man. your life must be super exciting if you have these boring dreams.

@valyn: i'm telling you - if i ever have a crazy dream like @carina444, then it will be a miracle!

- dreamkastr post showing @valyn, standing in line at a grocery store for 17 minutes.

VIEW ALL COMMENTS

@amandaharris289: that was one of the most beautiful songs i've ever heard. simply incredible, @carina444.

@carina444: who knows where this stuff comes from! sometimes i surprise myself ...

@reij: from your soul, @carina444.

@carina444: aw, thank you, @reij

@amandaharris289: i feel like i save all of your posts. this one will go to the top of the list. speaking of lists ... your followers are growing! watch out, local celebrity!

@carina444: be cool, @amandaharris289. lol

- dreamkastr post showing @carina444 as a sound wave, traveling from a computer screen into the headphones of an older carina. upon impact, the head-phones turned into an intensely green foliage that wrapped itself around her, in a gentle way. green like a barely lit light bulb. carina held it in her ears like a baby. her eyes were closed, and she was peaceful. a song was playing. the kick drum sparked glowing yellow lights around the room.

"ARE YOU EVEN REAL?"

the comments come
before
i wake up
each morning:

"breathtaking."

"magical."

"are you even real?"

i read them all.

some of them linger.

THE PARADOX

somehow,
all of
this
feels
both
too
much
and

not
enough?

BETWEEN CLASSES

outside,
the courtyard smells
like wet grass
and metal.

rain from last night
still clings
to the benches.

i drag my fingers
through the drops,
draw circles,
wipe them away.

the air is noisy -
not from machines,

but bees
near the fence line,
alive and busy.

for a second,
i forget the screens,
the whispers,
the attention on me.

ENOUGH

our music club
meets in the library,
which also has the
sound archive that maya-zen
uses for their music.

its air is thick
with the scent
of old vinyl records,
cassette tapes, and CDs
from eras long gone.

maya-zen selects a sound sample
from the 1900s -
children playing in a park,
captured by an old tape machine.

i can't focus -
the pull of my online life
tugs at me.

i glance at my bag,
feeling guilty
for cheating
on this moment.

and i remember when
moments like these
used to be
enough.

@simonejones93: your dreams are always like poetry in motion, @carina444.

@carina444: thank you!

@blackfemme3121: seeing your posts makes me feel like i can do anything.

@carina444: that means so much to me, truly.

@artistline89: you've inspired my latest painting. i'll tag you when it's done!

- dreamkastr post showing @carina444 in a glowing field of purple wildflowers. each flower turns into a tiny bird, fluttering upward and leaving trails of light as she walks through the field, her hands grazing the petals.

REFLECTION IN THE GIRLS' ROOM

after music club,
i head to the bathroom
and catch someone staring -
a person i don't know,

her hair braided neatly,
her eyes wide
with something like awe.

"carina, right?" she says.

her voice wavers,
like she's not sure
if i'm real.

i nod,
and she grins.

"i just wanted to say...
you're amazing.
your dreams are amazing."

she rushes out
before i can respond,

but her words
stay with me all day.

LUNCHTIME GLOW

at lunch, i feel it -

the warmth of their eyes,
the way people turn
just to watch me walk by.

valyn teases me:
"you're practically
royalty now!"

maya-zen rolls their eyes,
but even they smile
when someone
at another table says,

"that last dream
was everything."

FOR THE GIRLS LIKE ME

one girl stops me
on the way to math class.

her skin is deep brown,
her hair coiled and curled like mine.

"i just wanted to say thank you,"
she says.

"for what?" i ask,
but she's already walking away,

smiling like i've given her
something i didn't know i had.

"SHE'S JUST LIKE US"

it happens in the hall -

a group of girls
huddled around
a holo-screen,
watching my latest post.

"she's so cool,"
one of them says.

another nods,
but adds,
"she's just like us."

the words
catch me off guard.

i didn't know
being seen
could connect me
to people this way ...

"WHAT IF THIS IS ENOUGH?"

valyn asks,
"do you think
it's always
going to be like this?"

i shrug,
but the question stays with me.
what if this is my calling - to pull beauty
from the darkness of sleep,

to show the world
what i see when i close my eyes?

what if my dreams
are more than just mine,

and they are
meant to be shared,
to inspire?

GOING HOME

the sky folds itself
into a silver evening.

the noise of school fades,
replaced by the quiet pattern
of houses.

through the dome,
the stars
seem brighter
than usual.

home is a door
i open gently,

hoping today's version of me
still fits inside.

MAMA JEANIE'S STORY

"mama, tell me again
about my grandmother?"
i say, curled beside her
on the couch.

she smiles,
her hands
weaving through
my curly hair.

"our tribe
chose to believe,"
she says.

"while others
clung to the past,
we saw the future.

we knew
there was no going back,
no undoing
what they taught us.

your grandmother
fought in the war.

she carried messages
through the forests,
protected by shadows."

i imagine
my grandmother
- eyes fierce,
voice steady.

"do you think they'd
be proud of us now?"
i ask.

her smile falters.

"i think they'd wonder
what we've done
with the gifts
they gave us."

PROGRESS AND DISTANCE

sometimes,
i wonder if progress
is just another word
for distance.

the climate dome
protects us,
but it keeps us
from the stars.

dreamkastr connects us,
but it pulls us away
from our real lives.

even the absence
of disease
feels strange,

like we've traded pain
for something quieter,
but just as damaging.

INHERITANCE

i imagine my grandmother
lifting her face to real rain.
and i promise her -

i'll find a way
to feel
the real sky
again.

VIEW ALL COMMENTS

@daydreamer99: this is like... next level.

@carina444: i still don't know where these come from.
it's wild!

@reij: they come from you, carina. they *are* you.

- dreamkastr post showing @carina444 ascending a floating staircase made of translucent, glowing cubes. each step dissolves into a ripple of shimmering light as she moves upward, leaving a trail of iridescent mist behind her. above her, the sky shifts colors like an oil slick, and faint constellations rearrange themselves to form new patterns with every step. in the distance, a massive golden eye watches, blinking slowly, radiating warmth.

MONDAY

234 followers

TUESDAY

2,047 followers

WEDNESDAY

9,043 followers (!)

THURSDAY

19,098 followers?

FRIDAY

52,312 followers!

ENDORPHIN MACHINES

there's a rush
when the
notification pings.

a tiny spark,
like lighting a match.

the numbers climb,
and my heart races
as if i've caught
the attention
of the universe itself.

but the shine
fades quickly,
leaving shadows
that whisper:

"what if
you can't
keep up?"

VIEW ALL COMMENTS

@carina444: ha! my friend, you are the king of dreamkastr.

@valyn: yeah, @carina444, riveting dream, huh?!?

@carina444: this might be
my favorite dreamkastr post of all time.

@valyn: are you sure you don't want me to take over your account?

@carina444: lol. i'll let you know.

@valyn: maya-zen is missing a lot of this fun, aren't they?

@carina444: they are!

- dreamkastr post showing @valyn, brushing his teeth, in a bathroom. all white walls.

MAYA-ZEN'S WORLD

after school
we go to maya-zen's house
and hang out
in their room.

there's a lot of plants
swaying in the breeze
of an open window,

and the gentle hum
of their latest track -
ambient, ethereal,
as if the air itself were singing.

"you could post this,"
i tell them.

they shake their head,
their voice steady.

"not everything
needs to be shared."

THE DARKNESS IN THE MUSIC

maya-zen looks
out the window
and says,

"it's where i put
my depression.

in the music.
it's the only place
where it doesn't eat me."

their hands hover
above the keyboard,
building a sound

that feels like thunder
holding hands
with rain.

"people call it dark,"
they smile,
"but darkness
is just depth.
and in there
i can breathe."

THE UNIVERSE IN HER LAUGH

i head home after
maya-zen's house
and notice how
mama zara's laugh
could create
its own constellation.

it starts
from a single spark,
then spreads
across the room,
lighting everything it touches.

she says
i remind her
of the stars she loves.

"keep yourself grounded
through all of this, carina.

sleep used to be
the only thing
ego couldn't touch.

try not to let
this take over your life."

NIGHTTIME CLARITY

after mama's talk,
i sit with my journal,
its pages open,
inviting me to slow down.

her words linger:
"dreams are powerful,
but they don't define you."

i trace the edges
of the dreamkastr,
its screen dark,
but its presence loud.

it's been fun,
but maybe
it's time
to let it fade.

at least,
temporarily.

i'll keep tonight's dream
in my head
and won't watch it
on dreamkastr until
tomorrow night.

i won't
bring it
to school.

IN THE DARK

the house sleeps,
but my mind doesn't.

the pulse
of my own thoughts

seem to have
no end,
no real melody.

i put it all
in my journal

then fall asleep.

THE DREAM

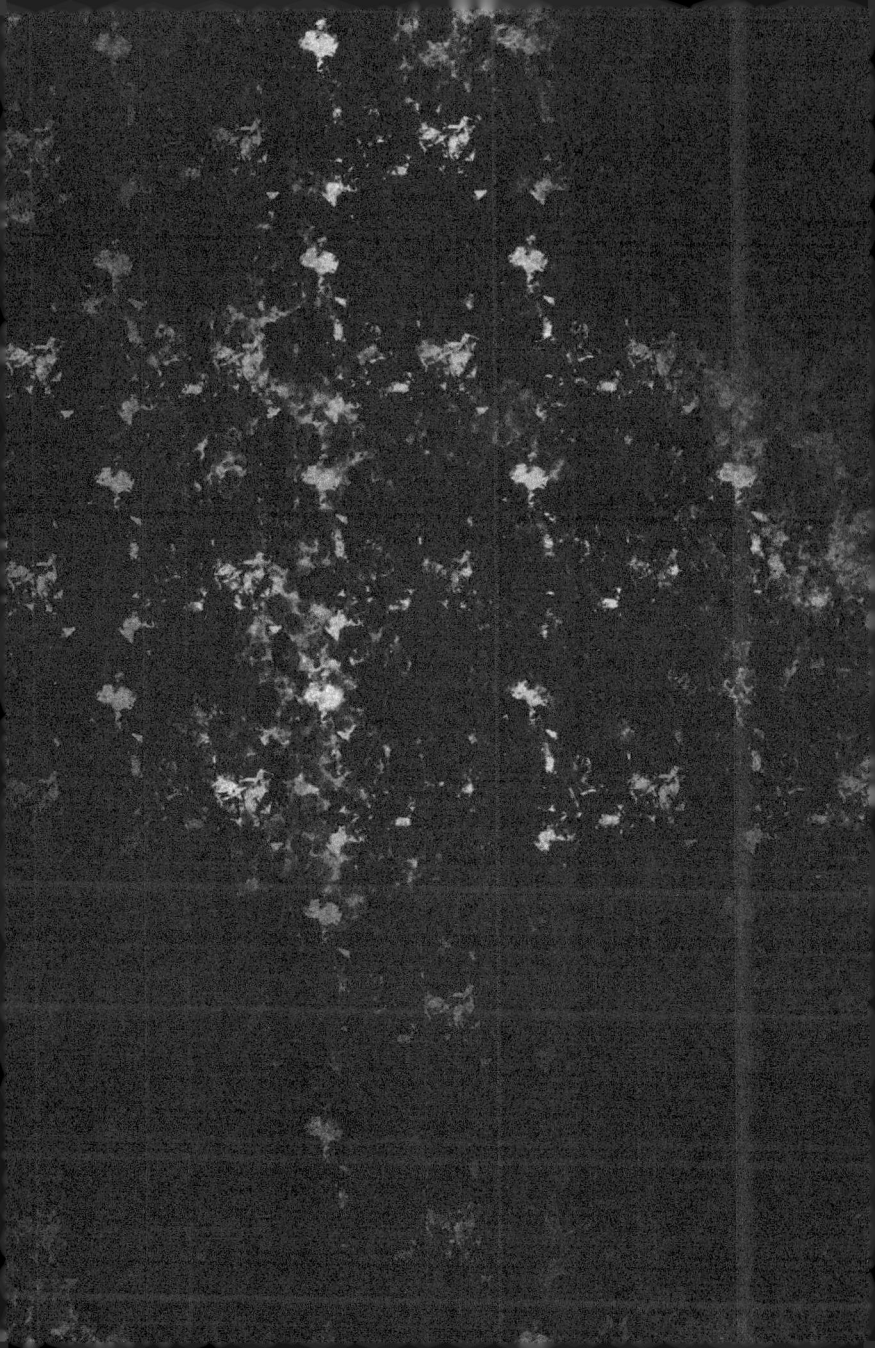

STILL IN THE DREAM ...

THE MORNING AFTER

i woke up gasping,
the dream
clinging to me
like a second skin,
damp and dark.

the air in my room
felt hollow -

too thick,
like i had
brought the fog
back with me.

my chest ached,
as if the dream
had stolen my breath

and forgotten to return it.

i sat up slowly,
my fingers trembling
as i reached
for the journal,
then stopped.

how do you write
about something

you don't
understand?

THE TASTE OF FEAR

my throat was dry,
my heartbeat loud,
a drum in the quiet
of the early morning.

for a moment,
i thought
the fog was still here,

lingering
in the corners
of my room.

it took me
a few minutes
to realize it wasn't.

but even then,
the fear stayed.

i didn't turn on
the dreamkastr.

i didn't want
to know if it had seen
what i just escaped.

(ANOTHER DETAIL)

the sky was
... wrong.

it was dark
all around me,

but
it was also

missing.

MORNING

i'm too worn out
to eat breakfast.

i avoid the family
and head out the door quickly.

maybe laughter
will find me at school.

ARE YOU OKAY?

the first thing i hear
when i step
into homeroom is:

"are you okay?"
from maya-zen.

"i'm fine,"
i say,

but the words
feel breakable.

"last night's dream was...
 intense," someone whispers,
their voice
dripping with hesitation.

"it wasn't
like your others,"
they say,
and i know
they're trying
to be polite.

i nod in silence,
even though
i want to scream.

WHAT AN INTERESTING LUNCH TRAY

at lunch,
valyn opens his mouth
like he wants to joke,
but the words die before they leave.

"that dream…"
he starts,
but his voice trails off,
hovering between us
like something fragile.

"can we not?"
i say, too quickly,
my tone
sharper than i intended.

his eyes widen,
but he doesn't push.

i look away,
pretending my tray
is suddenly interesting.

he just looks at me,
like he's trying to
figure out
if i've become
a stranger
overnight.

FOUR PINK MOONS

maya-zen slides
into the seat beside me,

their headphones
draped around their neck.

"carina ... about the dream.
want to talk?"

i stay silent.

"it's okay if you don't.
but i made something
for you," they say,

pulling out their tablet.
a slow beat fills the air -

melodic, strange,
warm.

"it's called
'four pink moons.'
i started it because
i was inspired
by that one
dream you had -
the first one
you showed us."

GIFT

i close my eyes,
letting the
strange and warm notes
wrap around me,

each one
somehow
whispering
that i'm not alone.

there's an echo of children
playing

and i feel lighter.

"i wanted it to feel
like a warm hug.
sorry if it's
a little dark.
it's all
i know
how to do."

HABIT

the streets blur
as i walk home,
the rhythm
of my footsteps
the only sound
i let myself hear.

the city
moves around me -
buses move
holograms flicker,
people pass by,
their faces open
and unaware
of the storm
inside me.

i clutch my bag tightly,
and then remember
that i left
the dreamkastr
at home.

i almost
forgot about
that dream
i had last night.

i definitely don't want
to see it or *feel* it
again.

CUTTING THROUGH THE CHILL

mama jeanie
greets me at the door,
her eyes searching.

"rough day?"
she asks. i nod,
but i don't say more.

i can feel her waiting,
but the words i need
stay trapped in my throat.

i can't tell her.
not this time.

she squeezes
my shoulder,
her warmth cutting
through the chill
of my thoughts,
and i fight back tears.

MAMA ZARA'S EYES

mama zara
glances up
from her tablet
as i pass.

her eyes catch mine -
sharp, knowing,
like she can see
the dark cloud
i'm trying to hide.

"you okay?" she asks,
and the words feel too big,
too hard to answer.

"i'm fine," i say,
 but even i don't believe it.

THE DEBATE

in my room,
the dreamkastr
sits on my desk, silent,
but louder than it's ever been.

i stare at it,
the light
i've come to love
now a quiet threat.

do i press play?

do i let myself
relive whatever that was?

or do i leave it,
let the darkness
stay locked inside
where it can't reach me?

i climb into bed,
turn my back
to the screen.

not tonight.

i need to rest
and not relive
that nightmare.

PEN TO PAPER

today felt like
walking through
a fog made of echoes.

everyone's voices
still in my head,
even when they're not near.

so i write -
not to explain,
but to empty.

each line a breath,
each breath a letting go.

if tonight brings a dream,
i hope it's quiet.

(THAT NIGHT'S DREAM)

i'm older,
sitting on a throne
made of bright screens.

around me
are the rhythm
of voices chanting my name:
"carina! carina!"

in my lap,
a journal lies open,
its pages filled
with my own
handwriting -

words i don't
remember writing
but seeing in front of me,
clearly.

valyn's name is scrawled
in bold, messy letters.

next to it:
"he's not funny. he's boring.
his dreams are ridiculous
and he wishes
he were as cool as me."

i flip the page,
my breath
catching up
with the anxiety.

maya-zen's name appears,
their music
reduced to a single sentence:

*"it's tedious,
like listening to static.
they think they're deep,
but it's nothing special."*

i try to close the journal,
but my hands won't obey.

the words are alive,
blazing on the page,
louder than i can bear.

the crowd loves me.

the journal burns in my hands,
its pages turning to ash
as the dream dissolves
into nothingness.

BETWEEN

i
wake ...
but
i
don't.

the
room
is
quiet,

but
my
chest
isn't.

i reach
for
myself
in
the
dark
and

miss.

AUTOMATIC UPLOAD

i open my eyes,
trembling.

the dream
still clawing at me,
its words
etched into my mind
like scars i can't rub away.

my journal, their faces,
their voices -
the betrayal i didn't choose
but somehow created.

i know it's out there.

the upload
is automatic.

dreamkastr
never waits.

i can't breathe.

what if they see it?

what if they believe it?

THE WALK TO SCHOOL

the morning
looks normal.

kids laugh,
the dome shines,
sparks skip
across the pavement.

but everything
feels tilted,

like the world
is slightly off-key.

i keep walking,
pretending
my heartbeat
isn't too loud.

pretending
i don't see
their faces
in every reflection.

pretending
i'm still me.

AFTERTASTE

nightmares
don't end
when you wake.

they cling -
in the throat,
in the breath,
in the spaces
between words.

i taste guilt
like metal.

i chew on silence
until it dissolves,
but it never does.

WHAT IF IT'S TRUE

what if
the dream
wasn't lying?

what if
some part of me

believes
every cruel word

i wrote
in that fire?

EMPTY SEATS

in homeroom,
their seats are empty.

i glance at the door,
again and again,
hoping they'll walk in,
that their smiles
will still be meant for me.

but the bell rings,
and i'm left
staring at the
empty desks.

their absence louder
than any words
they could
have spoken.

WHISPERS IN THE HALL

the hallways
are rivers of noise,
but every ripple seems
to carry my name.

"did you see it?"

"she's a weirdo."

"her friends must hate her now."

their words wrap around me,
tight and unrelenting.

i keep my head down,
but it doesn't help.

i feel exposed in a way
i didn't think
was possible.

ERASER / THE LONGEST DAY

i didn't see them all day.
the minutes crawl by,
each one heavier
than the last.

i check the places
we always meet - the library,
the back steps,
the lunchroom.

they're nowhere,
and i feel
like i've been erased.

i wish i could
erase my dreams.

WALKING HOME

the walk home
feels endless.

the air
presses
down on me,
too thick,
too loud,

like the whole city
knows what i've done.

each step
feels heavier
than the last.
and slower.

the whole earth
can't keep me
from falling apart.

ALONE

mama zara
and mama jeanie
are out with friends tonight,

and i'm thankful
to be home alone.

i sit at my desk,
the dreamkastr
glowing faintly.

i turn it on,
my fingers shaking.

YES.

i've lost a lot of
followers.

and there's hate-filled
unread messages
from strangers.

one tap.

two taps.

*are you sure you want
to delete your profile?*

i don't hesitate.

"yes."

the screen goes black,
and it's all gone.

the silence
after i delete it

is the loudest sound
i've ever heard.

AFTERMATH

the screen is dark,
the silence is suffocating.

for a moment,
i expect to feel free,

like i've escaped
something
i couldn't control.

but instead,
i feel like
i've erased a part of myself
i may never get back.

and i smash
the device on the ground,
glass everywhere.

my heart,
in pieces.

CHAPTER THREE:
TRANSFORMATION

THE MORNING AFTER ...

REBUILDING THE SKY

there were no dreams
last night,
and i was grateful
for the emptiness.

i needed silence.

just me
and my journal,
like it used to be.

still,
every line i write
spells their names.

valyn.

maya-zen.

the air feels smaller
without them in it.

how do you
rebuild the sky
after it's
been cracked?

PUT PEN TO PAPER

she finds me
in the kitchen,
half-awake,
half-broken.

"baby," she says,
"pain has to land somewhere."

i stare at the wall.

"then where should i put it?"
i whisper.

"do what you know
how to do best,"
she says.

"write them both a letter.
take a page
from your journal,
one that already knows
your fingerprints,
and let it speak
for you."

i nod,
but my chest tightens.

"what if they don't read it?"

mama zara
touches my arm,

"words always find
their way home."

QUIET WHERE THEY SHOULD BE

mama zara
drove me
to school because
i was too anxious
to walk.

i pass by
the library window,

it's empty.

it's a quiet
i don't know
how to fill.

AVOIDING EVERYONE

i walk the long way
toward class,

avoiding every hallway
that might bring me near
to anyone.

it's cowardly,
but i can't bear
to be around people.

i can hardly bear
to be around
myself.

i think
i'm going
to skip class
and write
the letters.

JOURNALING ALONE

my journal
sits open on a desk
in the library,
its pages blank.

i want to write,
to pour myself into words
like i used to.

but the sentences
feel too sharp.

so i close it.
leave it there.

wait for the
courage to come back.

A BREATH

i then
remember
to following my breath,
quiet down,
and empty.

doing that
lets the fire
hold my thoughts
calmly.

rebirth
starts
quietly.

somehow i know
this is the moment.

i am ready
to work
with the pain,

i'm also ready
to have my friends
back.

A LETTER TO VALYN

valyn,

i know i messed up,
and i'm not sure
if there's a way
to make this right.

i never thought
my dreams
would hurt you.
i never thought
they could
hurt anyone.

but they did,
and i'm sorry.

you're one of my best friends,
and the last thing
i'd ever want
is for you to think
i see you
as anything less
than brilliant.

i miss your jokes,
your way of making
even the worst days
a little brighter.
i miss you.

i hope someday
you can forgive me.

- carina

A LETTER TO MAYA-ZEN

maya-zen,

i don't know where to start.
i feel like every word
i could say
is too small
to carry the weight
of how sorry i am.

i didn't mean
for the dream
to say anything
about you,
about us.

but it did.
and i know
i hurt you.

your music
isn't just beautiful -
it's magic.

it's the quiet current
that keeps me grounded,
even when i'm falling apart.

i miss the way
you made silence feel
like a gift.

i miss you.

if there's any way
to rebuild this,
i'm willing to try.

- *carina*

MESSAGES RECEIVED

i leave the letters
on their desks in homeroom,
folded neatly,
their names written
on the outside.

by lunchtime,
they are
gone.

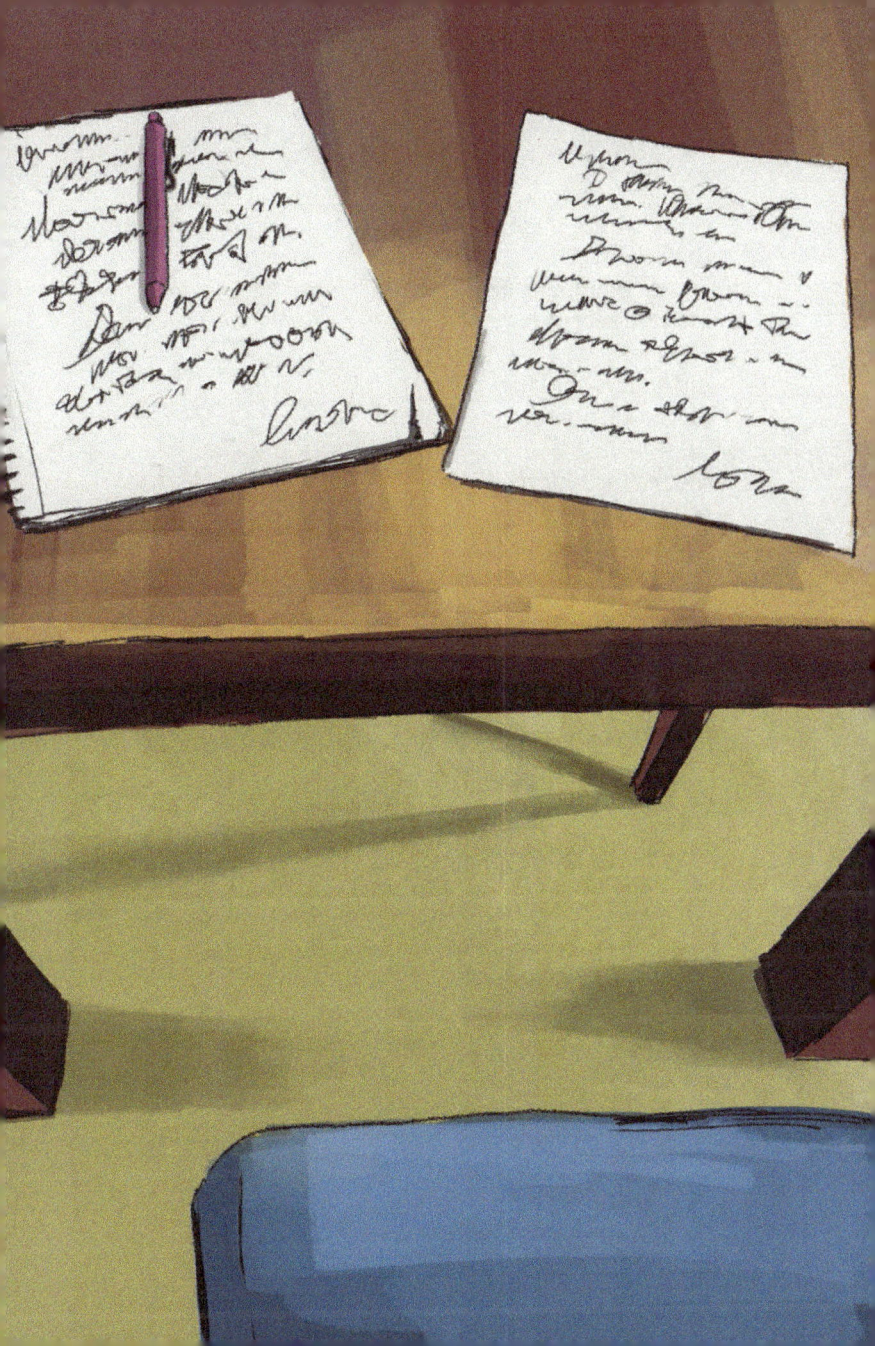

EMDR

that night,
i type "therapists near me"
into the search bar,

my fingers shaking
on the keyboard.

the results blur together,
rows of smiling faces
and calm descriptions
that feel too distant
to be real.

i click the first name
that feels gentle enough
to hold me:

dr. ruthie voss.

HEALING

that night,
mama jeanie
reminds me,

"when diseases vanished in 2077,
doctors turned inward,
mapping the mind
instead of the veins.

you made a good choice
to seek help
navigating
your emotions.

i never thought
this would happen
in my lifetime,
but here we are."

we'll go to
dr. voss' office
after school tomorrow.

BEAUTIFUL AGAIN

that night
i dreamt of a river
made of gold.

its current was protective,
carrying me gently,
rich against my skin.

for the first time
in weeks,
my dream
didn't scare me.

it was
beautiful again.

but i'm dreading
going to school ...

THE WHISPER CAMPAIGN

back at school,
the whispers follow me
like shadows,

pulling at the edges
of my day.

"she thinks
she's better
than us now."

"didn't she
delete everything?"

"her dreams
were probably fake anyway."

each cold word
sticks to my skin.

i keep walking,
but my steps
feel smaller

because i'm missing
my friends,
my anchors,
so much.

CORNERED

by the lockers,
they block my way -
two girls i barely know,
their faces sharp with something
i can't name.

"your dreams
weren't even that good,"
one of them says,
her tone a dagger
disguised as a smile.

the other laughs,
leaning in.

"who quits when they're famous?
what's wrong with you?"

i want to say something,
but the words crumble
before they reach my tongue.

i turn and walk away,
their laughter following me.

UNREAD (2)

i walk faster,
like distance
can save me.

their laughter
still clings
to my back.

but then -
a flicker of something
soft.
two envelopes,
slipped between
the slats of my locker.

my name is written
on both of them.

the handwriting so familiar
that my heart aches

and leaps
at the same time.

VALYN'S LETTER

carina,

i was angry,
but i never stopped
being your friend.

i know you didn't mean
what the dream said.

dreams are weird, right?
they pull at the parts of us
we don't want to face.

you're still the same carina -
the one who laughs at
my dumb jokes
and makes the world brighter.

i miss you.

and admit it -
you miss hearing about
my *amazing* dreams.

let's fix this.

- *valyn*

MAYA-ZEN'S LETTER

carina,

dreams are messy,
but so is life.

i'm still mad.
not at the dream,
but at the space
it put between us.

i want to find my way back
to where we were -

the library, the music,
the quiet we made together.

i think we can.

- maya-zen

OPEN AGAIN

i read them both
twice.

the words
are steady
with my
heartbeat.

my chest
loosens.

the air
feels easier
to breathe.

forgiveness
is a quiet
return
to myself.

THREADS

friendship
is a fragile thread -

but threads,
when woven together
can carry
the weight of us.

and maybe
that's what maya-zen,
valyn, and i are:

a fabric
stitched with silence,
with laughter,
with pain,
and with forgiveness.

THE PATH TO DR. VOSS

the city ends
where the trees begin.

we board the
busy public transit
to head to dr. voss'
office.

no one says much.

the silence feels like
permission.

we get off
at our exit
and walk down
a narrow road
lined with wildflowers
and old wooden signs -

no screens,
no humming drones,
just the sound
of gravel under tires.

part of me
wants to turn back,
but the
air smells cleaner here,
more alive.

THE IN-BETWEEN

the city moves on
frantically
as we ride.

i watch trees
replace buildings,
and for once,
the silence
feels good.

i don't know
what to expect,

but something
in me
is ready
to listen.

DR. RUTHIE VOSS

her office is a quiet rebellion
against the energy of the city,
much like maya-zen's house.

there's
the scent
of sage,

and a row of crystals
playing with the sun.

dr. voss greets us
on a porch covered
in ivy and windchimes.

mama jeanie and mama zara
hug me once more
before heading to the garden.

she greets me
with a calm smile,
her voice
smooth as poetry.

her locs, long and flowing,
touching the ground when
she's in a chair.

"carina," she says,
as if she already knows me.

THE BUZZERS

the room smells
like rain and rosemary.

books stacked high,
a window cracked
just enough for birdsong.

she smiles
and simply says
"you are safe here."

dr. voss places small buzzers
in my hands,
each one pulsing gently,
first on the left,
then the right.

"follow the rhythm,"
she says.

it's strange at first,
but soon my mind
feels quieter,
the storm softening
with every pulse.

"I'VE HEARD OF YOU"

dr. voss leans forward,
her eyes sharp with curiosity.

"you were quite the presence
on dreamkastr,"
she says.

i stiffen,
the words
catching me off guard.

she smiles gently.
"i study dreams, carina.
and yours…"

she pauses,
choosing her words carefully.
"yours are
something special."

"dreams are blueprints,"
dr. voss says,
"not of what will happen,
but of who you are
becoming.

they reveal the fractures,
the hidden colors,
the echoes we carry
when the world
isn't looking."

her words
rest perfectly
in the air.

for the first time
in weeks,
i feel like my own mind
is a place i can trust

and a place
i can rest in.

INFINITE

dr. voss asks me
to describe my dreams.

the ones from before -
the ones that felt like art.

i close my eyes,
the buzzers
pulsing steadily in my hands,
and let the words
spill out:

"a staircase of glowing cubes.
a sky of shifting constellations.
a river of golden light."

she nods,
her gaze steady.
"and how did those dreams
make you feel?"

"like i was infinite,"
i say.

NO DREAM TONIGHT

the house
is quiet
when we get home.

mama jeanie
lights a candle,
the smell of cedar
in the air.
i fall into bed

expecting color,
sound,
a sky that bends.

but nothing happens
except a deep sleep.

quiet.

LETTING THE JOY IN

for the first
time
in what feels
like forever,

my breath
passes
through
my lungs
with such
perfection

that everything
arounds me
feels almost ...

peaceful.

STRENGTH IN SILENCE

that night,
i write it down
in my journal:

the hateful words
of others,

the laughter,

the way
it all made me
feel small.

and then i write:

"i am more
than their whispers."

it doesn't erase the hurt,
but it feels like reclaiming
a piece of myself
that feels like
it was taken away.

FLOWER/BLOOM

that night,
i dreamt of a garden.

its flowers blooming
with every step i took.

the air was alive with music,
and the stars above
danced to a rhythm
i couldn't name.

when i woke,
the dream
stayed with me,

and it felt good
to only have it
in my head.

THE DOOR

morning comes
without hurry.

i sit up,
breathe deep,
and feel
steady.

today
i walk
instead of hide.

when i open
the door,
they're there -

valyn
and maya-zen!

no words.

just a hug
that feels
like love.

THE LONG WALK BACK

we walk to school
together,

unsure
where to start.

the air
between us
is thin
but calm.

valyn's smile is back
and i missed it so much.

maya-zen also smiles,
says they wrote
a new song -
"tiny data fossils."

"i filled it with
strange samples
and tried to make it groovy,"
they laugh.

"pretty sure
you two
are the only ones
who'll ever listen."

we laugh,
and it feels
like a beginning.

THEIR SMILES AGAIN

in the lunchroom,
they sit across from me,
their smiles tentative,
but real.

i feel it again -
that warmth,
that sense
of being whole.

A MOMENT IN THE LIBRARY

we sit together
at our usual table,
the quiet filling the space
where words used to stumble.

the silence between us
feels like static before a song.

it feels like something new -
like the start of something
we didn't know
we could still have.

a deepening.

BACK AGAIN

after school,
i head back
to dr. voss' office,

the buzzers pulse,
first left,
then right,
the rhythm steady,
calming.

dr. voss asks,
"how do you feel,
when the dreams return?"

"lighter," i say.
"like i'm finding my way
back to myself."

WHAT THE CRYSTALS SAY

the crystals
that line dr. voss' office
catches the sun's reflection
in a way that feels intentional.

"do they mean something?"
i ask,
watching her hands
move over the smooth surfaces.

"they're grounding,"
she says.

"they remind me
that even in chaos,
there is clarity.

your dreams
are like that, too.
there's clarity
in all of them.

allow yourself
permission
to see the whole
picture."

COMING IN HOT

dr. voss hands
me a notebook,
its pages blank
but full of possibility.

"write what you feel,"
she says.
"not what you *think*
you should feel."

the first word i write is "lost."
the second is "found."

i'm a hot mess!

THE FRAGILITY OF FORGIVENESS

and then
a new poem
came to me
about my friendship
with valyn and maya-zen.

it's called "glass"

"GLASS"

forgiveness feels
like a glass bridge -
beautiful,
but terrifying to cross.

every apology reflects back at me,
distorted by the cracks i can't repair.

i feel your compassion again,
but i tread lightly,
unsure if one wrong step
might shatter it all

or one bad dream
would trip us up
and worsen
the fall.

BLINK

back in therapy,
dr. voss asks me
to read "glass."

she also
asks me to
talk about
the blackbird dream.

the one with
the shifting moons.

i still
think about
that one a lot.

ironically,
i wish i could
see it again.

"maybe you can
see it again.
all of it, in vivid detail."
dr. voss says.
"i think
you are ready."

TRUST

but how?

i smashed my
dreamkastr.

"wait. does dreamkastr
store dreams
somewhere? i don't
want to relive
all of those moments!
i will not get back
on there!"

"carina. take a breath.
there is calm
within you.
flow, don't fight,"
dr. voss says.

"there is calm
within me"
i say.

"flow,
don't fight."

THE CALM WITHIN

inhale.

the storm bends.

exhale.

the world feels more gentle.

somewhere between
the inhale and the exhale
is me -

steady,
like the keel
of a ship
named carina.

ANOTHER PERSON'S DREAM

dr. voss says
"carina,
once i dreamt
of a library
made of clouds.

every dream
i ever had
was filed
on a shelf
of stars.

i tried to
read them all,
but the pages
turned themselves.

when
i woke up,
i somehow
knew
that memory
is its own
kind of dream."

QUANTUM

dr. voss
leans back in her chair,
her locs
catching the sunlight.

"there's something
i've been meaning
to tell you,"
she says,
her voice calm,
but charged.

"i think you are
now ready
to hear this:

you aren't
the only one
who's had
these dreams."

i stare at her,
the words settling over me
like a second skin.

"what do you mean?" i ask,
my voice shaking.

ENTANGLEMENT

dr. voss
smiles.

"i mean,
i can give you
your dreams back
and help you see
them differently.

i know someone
who's had
the exact
same ones."

dr. voss asks,

"do you want
to meet them?"

**listen to
the music of
maya-zen!**

"you hold the sound of the future in yr hands"

THE AUTHOR, GRAPHIC DESIGNER & MUSICIAN

MARCUS AMAKER

@ @CHARLESTONPOET

MARCUS AMAKER is a dad, husband, and the first Poet Laureate of Charleston, SC. He's an award-winning poet, musician, and opera librettist whose work has been recognized by the Kennedy Center, NPR, PBS, and more. He has published 12 of his own books, released over 45 albums of music, and leads workshops for writers of all ages. In 2024, he was inducted into the S.C. Literary Hall of Fame and included on a list of favorite poets in America by Literary Hub and WildSam. Most importantly, he takes daily naps.

THE ILLUSTRATOR

GEOFFREY CHANDLER

@ @GEOFFP_ARTY_USA

GEOFFREY CHANDLER is a dad, husband, and illustrator living in North Carolina. The son of a writer and a librarian, he loves bringing stories to life through art. When he's not drawing, he's marveling at the talents of his friends and family, tolerating his mischievous dog, and reminding others that creativity is about joy, not perfection.

OTHER WORKS
BY MARCUS AMAKER

BOOKS!

Listening To Static *(2005)*
Poems For Augustine *(2005)*
The Soft Paper Cut *(2007)*
The Present Presence *(2012)*
The Spoken Word. Selected
Poems: 2003 - 13 *(2013)*
Mantra: An Interactive
Poetry Book *(2015)*

Empath (2017)
The Birth of All Things *(2020)*
Black Music Is *(2021)*
Hold What Makes You Whole
(2023)
we deserve a world without
war *(2025)*

MARCUSAMAKER.COM

OPERA!

Unknown *(2021)*
*with composer Shawn E.
Okpebholo // UrbanArias –
Arlington, VA*

The Weight of Light *(2024)* –
*with composer Gillian Rae
Perry // Chicago Opera The-
ater – Chicago, IL*

Singers and Stanzas *(2024)* //
HALO – Charleston, SC

Climate Change Choral Project
(2027) // *Baltimore, MD;
Detroit, MI; Seattle, WA; TBA,
CT; and Chicago, IL.*

MUSIC!

Big Butt *(1986)*
Gimme Some *(1987)*
Play It *(1988)*
Say No! *(1988)*
Daydreamin' *(1988)*
All Uv the Time *(1989)*
Minimalism *(2005)*
Dealate *(2005)*
Escapism *(2006)*
1945 *(2008)*
Lady Phoenix *(2009)*
Digital Detox *(2010)*
The Cassette Demos *(2011)*
Sunday Rain *(2011)*
Animation *(2012)*
The New Foundation
(with Quentin E. Baxter)
(2014)
The Drum Machine, Part 1
(2015)
Analogue // 1 - 6 *(2016–17)*
Telemaque. *(2017)*
Empath
(with Quentin E. Baxter)
(2018)
Open EP *(2018)*
Empath (Variations) *(2018)*
Creating Empty Space *(2019)*
The Birth of All Things *(2019)*
The Weight That Holds

the Animal *(2019)*
Rei *(2019)*
Contagion *(2020)*
Rhythm Vaccine *(2020)*
subversive *(2020)*
Muscle Memory
(with Quentin E. Baxter)
(2021)
TEXTURE // 1
(with Concept RXCH) (2021)
ELECTROPOEMS *(2022)*
kept & let go of *(2022)*
flushed & in bloom EP *(2022)*
humid tombstones *(2023)*
tape loop live: tua lingua,
march 16, 2024
tape loop live: local 616,
march 23, 2024
earth poems *(2024)*
9 letters to artificial intelli-
gence (EP) *(2024)*
threshold 1–3 *(2024)*
TEXTURE // 2
(with Concept RXCH)
(2025)
dust, kick, and snare *(2025)*
you hold the sound of the
future in yr hands
(as maya-zen) (2025)
melt. *(2026)*

TAPELOOP.BANDCAMP.COM